This book belongs to

. . . .

Front endpapers by Charlie-Marco Jarvis aged 7 (left) and Olivia Preston aged 7 (right)
Back endpapers by Jenny Stowe aged 7 (left) and Bailey Forbes aged 7 (right)

A big thank you to Princethorpe Infant School, Birmingham for helping with the endpapers—K.P.

For Summer, Charlie and Miles—V.T.

For Zoe Tzannes—now every day is a Zoe Day!—K.P.

OXFORD
UNIVERSITY PRESS

Great Clarendon Street, Oxford OX2 6DP

Oxford University Press is a department of the University of Oxford.
It furthers the University's objective of excellence in research, scholarship,
and education by publishing worldwide. Oxford is a registered trade mark of
Oxford University Press in the UK and in certain other countries

First published 2015
First published in paperback 2016

British Library Cataloguing in Publication Data available

ISBN: 978-0-19-274406-7 (hardback)
ISBN: 978-0-19-274408-1 (paperback)
ISBN: 978-0-19-274407-4 (paperback with audio CD)

2 4 6 8 10 9 7 5 3 1

Printed in China

Paper used in the production of this book is a natural, recyclable product made
from wood grown in sustainable forests. The manufacturing process conforms
to the environmental regulations of the country of origin

www.winnie-the-witch.com

Valerie Thomas   Korky Paul

Winnie's Haunted House

OXFORD
UNIVERSITY PRESS

It was a lovely, warm,
sunny afternoon.
Winnie the Witch thought
she'd have a sleep.

She sat down in her big armchair,
shut her eyes, and in two minutes
she was snoring.

Wilbur, Winnie's big black cat,
thought he'd have a sleep, too.

He curled up on a cushion,
shut his eyes, and in three minutes . . .

a bumblebee flew in
through the window.

Wilbur liked to chase bumblebees.
He jumped up at the bumblebee,

BuzZZZZ!

and missed.

He jumped up again . . . higher . . .

missed the bumblebee . . .

and landed . . .

in the big vase of flowers
on Winnie's table.

CRASH! SMASH! SPLASH!

Winnie woke up.
'Oh no! My best vase!' she said.
'Did you do that, Wilbur?'
But she couldn't see
Wilbur anywhere.

'Where are my glasses?'
asked Winnie.
'Who took them?'

She bent down to look for them.

Wilbur shot out from
under Winnie's chair.
Where could he hide?

Behind the curtains.

SWISH! CRASH!

Down came the curtains, on top of Winnie.

'Blithering broomsticks!'
she shouted.
Winnie crawled out from
under the curtains.
'Who did that? Was it a ghost?
Is my house haunted?'

Wilbur raced up the stairs.
Where could he hide?

Then he saw the perfect place.
Winnie would never look up there.

Wilbur jumped onto the banister
and then sprang onto the chandelier.

The chandelier swung
from side to side.

Wilbur hung on tightly.

Perhaps the chandelier
wasn't a good idea.

Wilbur jumped back onto
the banister just in time.

CRASH!

It definitely wasn't a good idea.

Winnie rushed into the hall.
'My beautiful chandelier!'
she cried. 'My house *is* haunted.
There must be a spell to fix a
haunted house.'

Winnie picked up her Big Book of Spells and quickly turned over the pages. Yes, there it was: a spell for fixing a haunted house. Wasn't it? It was hard to read it without her glasses.

She shut her eyes, stamped her foot three times, waved her magic wand, and shouted,

Abracadabra!

There was a
great gust of wind
and everything went dark.
Owls and bats flew overhead.
Skeletons rattled on the staircases.
Spiders' webs hung from the ceilings,
thick with hairy spiders. Ghosts slithered
through the walls. **'Woo, wooo,'** they cried.
Winnie's house *really* was a haunted house.

Whoosh!

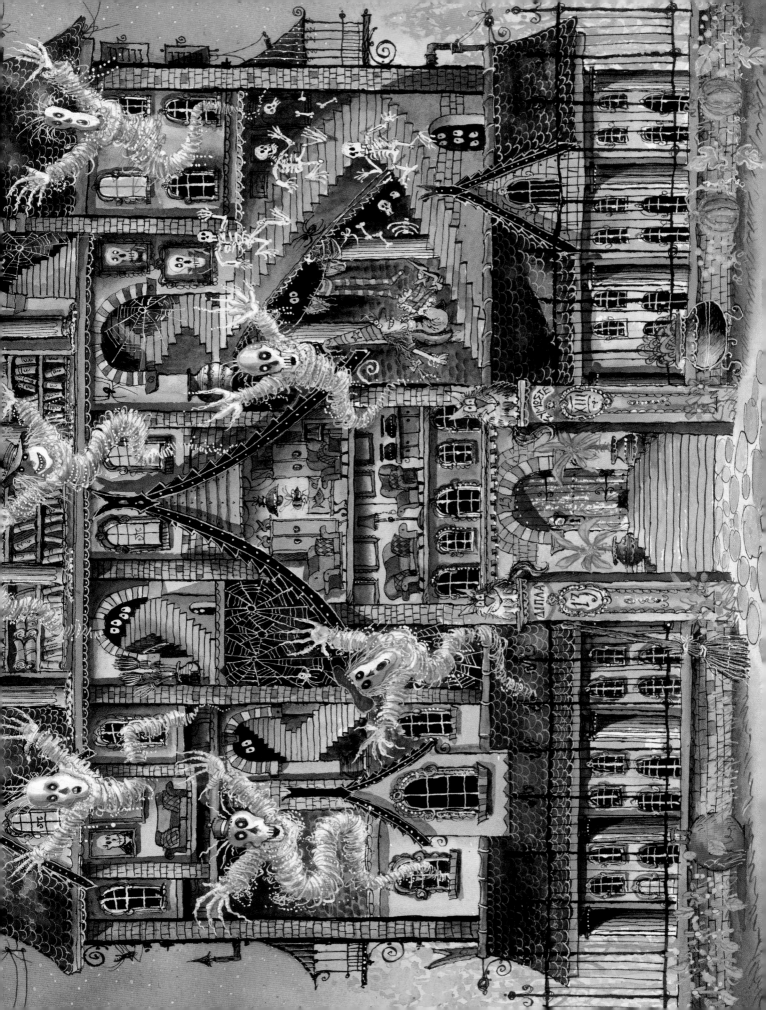

'**BOO!**'
shouted a ghost.
Winnie was very surprised.

She jumped back,
into a sticky spider's web.

A big hairy spider tickled her nose.

'Urk! Yuck! A-a-a-choOO!'

Wilbur came running down the stairs.
'Meeow, meeeow,' he cried.

'Don't be frightened, Wilbur,'
Winnie said. 'I must have made
a mistake with my spell.'

She looked in the Big Book of Spells again,
and a swooping owl knocked her glasses onto her nose.
'So that's where they were,' she said.
Winnie looked carefully at the spell.

It said:

To ✶MAKE☽ a Haunted House.

'Oh dear,'
said Winnie.
'I didn't see
to make.'

Winnie looked at the next spell.
It said:

To
FIX ☽ ★
a Haunted House
DO the haunting
spell backwards.

'That should work,'
Winnie said.

She opened her eyes wide,
waved her foot high in the air three times,
waved her wand backwards,
and shouted,

Arbadacarba!

WHOOSH!

All was quiet. Winnie's haunted house was
Winnie's house again. But it was a very messy house.

There were bits of vase,
heaps of curtains,
and chunks of chandelier
everywhere.

'Never mind,' Winnie said. 'I'll soon clean it up.'
She waved her magic wand, shouted,

Abracadabra!

. . . and the vase, the curtains, and the chandelier were as good as new.
'That's a very useful spell,' Winnie said.

Then Winnie sat down in an armchair.
She thought she'd finish her sleep.
Wilbur climbed onto her lap.
He really needed a sleep.

'We've had an exciting day, haven't we, Wilbur,' Winnie said. 'I don't suppose I'll ever know what *was* haunting my house.'

I hope not, Wilbur thought.
'**Purr, purr, purr,**' he said.